One of Anne's favorites!

BERNADETTE'S BUSY MORNING
ILA HODGSON

PICTURES BY JOHN E. JOHNSON

PARENTS' MAGAZINE PRESS • NEW YORK

To my daughter, Valerie,
who loves animals

Bernadette the circus bear woke up early. She stood up and stretched out her big brown arms. She felt fine and frisky.

Bernadette worked with Buffo, the clown, and slept outside Buffo's little white trailer. Her ankle was fastened with a chain to a stake in the ground. She had slept that way for as long as she could remember, and she did not at all mind the chain.

Buffo's trailer door was closed so she knew that he was still asleep. She scratched at the door with her big bear claws, but there was no sound from within.

She put her big bear mouth near the green door and said, "Gr-r-r-r. Gr-r-r-r. Gr-r-rand morning to get up."

Still, there was no sound from within. Buffo was sleeping soundly.

Bernadette began to dance around the stake in the ground. She hoped that her dancing would attract the notice of the two boys who were busily carrying huge buckets of water to the elephants. She was thirsty and wanted the boys to bring HER a bucket of cool water, too.

Ordinarily, the boys would have loved to watch Bernadette dancing. But yesterday the ringmaster had told them that if they did a good job of bringing water to the elephants, they could have tickets for the afternoon show. The boys were so busy doing a good job that they did not notice Bernadette, who was getting warmer and thirstier by the minute.

The lion trainer walked rapidly across the circus grounds.

"Gr-r-r-r. Gr-r-r-r. Gr-r-rand morning for a drink of water," Bernadette called after him. But the lion trainer had so many lions and tigers to take care of that he did not hear her.

She was still dancing about when, all of a sudden, SNAP went a weak link in her chain. She almost fell over backwards when the chain broke, but she soon steadied herself and looked down to see what had happened.

"Isn't that something!" she said, seeing that she was no longer fastened to the stake. "Now I'll just go get myself a drink of water."

She walked over to the long row of elephants. They were drinking from the buckets of water so she leaned down and took a drink, too. The elephants were kind and did not mind sharing their water.

Along came one of the boys with another bucket of water. He did not see Bernadette until he was almost on top of her.

"Help! Help!" he cried, dropping the bucket and spilling the water on Bernadette.

The icy water startled Bernadette and she began to run. The elephants were so frightened to see a big brown bear running and two boys screaming that they began to trumpet loudly through their long trunks.

Soon the whole circus was in an up-roar, but Bernadette did not wait to see what was happening. She kept right on running. She ran until she had left the circus grounds far behind and had come to a busy street.

"HONK! HONK!" the cars said to Bernadette.

"OOGA! OOGA!" the trucks said to Bernadette.

She said, "Gr-r-r-r!" to the cars and
trucks and did not cross the street. She
walked on the sidewalk trying to be
friendly with the people she met along
the way.

"Help! Help!" yelled the people and they ran in all directions.

Bernadette was still thirsty so she continued down the street looking for water.

Presently the sidewalk led to a little park with trees and grass and green benches. Near the entrance was a two-layer fountain with clear, flowing water.

A man was reading the morning newspaper on a bench near the fountain.

"Gr-r-rand morning," said Bernadette in a friendly way.

The man dropped his paper and jumped off the green bench. "Good grief!" he yelped, and ran right out of the little park.

Beside the fountain Bernadette saw two ladies feeding peanuts to some gray squirrels.

"Ah," she said hungrily. "I love peanuts." She hurried over and politely waited for the ladies to give her some.

"Goodness gracious!" cried the ladies. They dropped the peanuts and ran off.

Bernadette calmly picked up the bag of peanuts and ate what was left.

"Not much breakfast for a hungry bear," she mumbled as she gobbled them up.

By now the morning sun had climbed high into the blue sky. The day was getting warm, and the large bottom layer of the fountain looked cool and inviting. Bernadette got in and sat down. Water from the top layer flowed down on her head and made a good shower.

Bernadette splashed a lot and hummed a tune to herself. It went, "Gr-r-rand morning for a bath. Gra-la-la. Gra-la-la."

After her bath, however, Bernadette felt lonesome and hungry. Even the squirrels had run away, and she was all alone. She wondered if she would be able to get back to the circus.

Then she saw a crowd of people coming into the park. First came a big policeman with a blue uniform and brass buttons. Next came Buffo! Bernadette ran over and gave him a big wet bear hug.

"I've looked all over for you, Bernadette," he told her. She didn't understand every word he said, but she knew what he meant.

"Let's get away from the wet bear," said the people. Bernadette did not understand the words, but she knew what THEY meant, too.

All she wanted was to go home to the circus where no one ran away from her. Buffo had brought a rope to attach to her collar, and they walked back to the circus together.

The two boys who had been watering the elephants brought her a bucket of water. The lion trainer gave her a piece of meat he had saved from the lions' breakfast.

"Bernadette is back," one person told another. Everyone came to see her, and Bernadette was not lonesome anymore.

The sun was now high and hot in the blue sky. Bernadette curled up beside Buffo's little trailer for a nap.

"Gr-r-rand to be home," she said drowsily just before she went to sleep.